This book belongs to:

_____

_____

_____

First published 1999 by Walker Books Ltd
87 Vauxhall Walk, London SE11 5HJ

2 4 6 8 10 9 7 5 3 1

© 1999 Lucy Cousins

Based on the Audio Visual series "Maisy". A King Rollo Films Production for
PolyGram Visual Programming. Original script by Jeanne Willis.

This book has been typeset in Lucy Cousins typeface.

Printed in Hong Kong

British Library Cataloguing in Publication Data
A catalogue record for this book is
available from the British Library.

0-7445-6764-5 (hb)
0-7445-7215-0 (pb)

Maisy's Bedtime

Lucy Cousins

WALKER BOOKS
AND SUBSIDIARIES
LONDON • BOSTON • SYDNEY

It's bedtime for Maisy and Panda.

Maisy closes her bedroom curtains.

Tuwoo, tuwoo, says the owl.

Maisy has a wash
and brushes
her teeth.

Maisy puts on her pyjamas.

She gets into
bed and reads
a bedtime story.

But where
is Panda?

Is he in the toy box?

Oh, there he is!

Maisy switches off the light.

But she can't go to sleep.

Maisy needs
the loo!

So does Panda.

Maisy is really
sleepy now.

Good night, Maisy.
Good night, Panda.

If you're crazy for Maisy, you'll love these other books featuring Maisy and her friends.

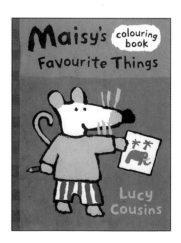

Other titles

Maisy's ABC • Maisy Goes to Bed • Maisy Goes to the Playground
Maisy Goes Swimming • Maisy Goes to Playschool
Maisy's House • Happy Birthday, Maisy • Maisy at the Farm